Clap Your Hands

Lorinda Bryan Cauley

PaperStar

The Putnam & Grosset Group

Copyright © 1992 by Lorinda Bryan Cauley
All rights reserved. This book, or parts thereof, may not be
reproduced in any form without permission in writing from the publisher.
A PaperStar Book, published in 1997 by The Putnam & Grosset Group,
345 Hudson Street, New York, New York 10014.
PaperStar is a registered trademark of The Putnam Berkley Group, Inc.
The PaperStar logo is a trademark of The Putnam Berkley Group, Inc.
Originally published in 1992 by G. P. Putnam's Sons.
Published simultaneously in Canada.
Manufactured in China

Library of Congress Cataloging-in-Publication Data
Cauley, Lorinda Bryan.
Clap your hands/by Lorinda Bryan Cauley.   p..   cm.
Summary: Rhyming text instructs the listener to
find something yellow, roar like a lion,
give a kiss, tell a secret, spin in a circle,
and perform other playful activities.
[1. Play—Fiction.   2. Stories in rhyme.]   I. Title.
PZ8.3.C3133C1.   1992   91-12863.   CIP.   AC.   [E]—dc20
ISBN 978-0-698-11428-9
38 39 40

To my little girls, Sean and Erin

Clap your hands,
stomp your feet.

Shake your arms,
then take a seat.

Rub your tummy,
pat your head.

Find something yellow,
find something red.

Reach for the sky,
wiggle your toes.

Stick out your tongue
and touch your nose.

Roar like a lion,
growl like a bear.

Give me a kiss…
Do you dare?

Wiggle your fingers,
slap your knee.

I'll tickle you
if you tickle me!

Find something big,
find something small.

Spin in a circle…
but try not to fall!

Close your eyes
and count to four.

Now do a somersault
across the floor.

Spread your feet,
look upside down.

Make a silly face
and act like a clown.

Hop like a bunny,
flap like a bird.

Quiet as a mouse, now...
Don't say a word!

Tell me your name.
How old are you?

Tell me a secret,
and I'll tell you one, too!

Purr like a kitten,
bark like a dog.

Crawl like a baby,
jump like a frog.

Count your fingers,
count your toes.

Wiggle your eyebrows,
wiggle your nose.

Show me a smile,
show me a frown.

Stand on one foot
and jump up and down.

Fly like an airplane
high in the sky.

It's time to go now,
so wave bye-bye...

Bye-bye!